Prints

written by
Judy Ann Sadler

illustrated by
Marilyn Mets

KIDS CAN PRESS LTD.

To my father and mother-in-law, Don and Barb Sadler,
for their time, love and support,
and for the most charming "prints" of all,
my husband, Jeff

First U.S. edition 1997 published by
Kids Can Press Ltd.
85 River Rock Drive,
Suite 202
Buffalo, NY 14207

Published in Canada by
Kids Can Press Ltd.
29 Birch Avenue
Toronto, Ontario, Canada
M4V 1E2

Edited by Laurie Wark
Designed by Nancy Ruth Jackson
Cover design by Karen Powers
Cover photos by Frank Baldasarra

Printed in Hong Kong by
Wing King Tong Co. Ltd.

92 0 9 8 7 6 5 4 3

Canadian Cataloguing in Publication Data

Sadler, Judy Ann, 1959—
    Prints

(Kids can easy crafts)
ISBN 1-55074-083-0

1. Prints — Technique — Juvenile literature.
I. Mets, Marilyn. II. Title. III. Series.

NE860.S33 1992 j760 C91-095551-4

CONTENTS

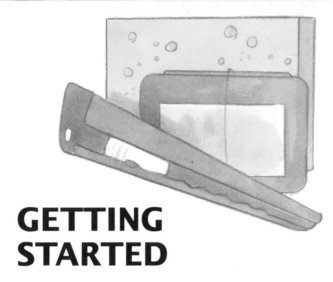

GETTING STARTED

Did you know you've been a printmaker all your life? You've left fingerprints on furniture, nose prints on windows and muddy footprints on floors! It was easy, wasn't it? But someone has probably wiped all those prints away. So how about making prints that will last? By using materials you have found, shaped or cut, you can create any printing design you like. Part of the charm of printmaking is that you never really know how it will look until you lift your print design off the paper. A favorite print can be repeated again and again, or change the color of paint or paper and your picture looks new!

This book will show you many different methods of printmaking and how to use them on all kinds of projects. Begin by gathering the materials you see on these pages and reading the helpful hints that go with them. Happy printing!

newspaper Always cover your work surface with newspaper before you begin. Also, it is helpful to have a couple of layers under your printing paper when you're stamping.

wet cloths and rags You'll want to keep your hands clean when you're printing so that you don't get fingerprints where you don't want them.

paint shirt This helps to keep your clothes clean.

paper Almost any kind of paper will work for printing. It's good to have scrap paper around too, so that you can test your printing method.

paint Liquid or powder tempera paint, poster paint or fabric paint all work well for printing. Pre-mixed liquid tempera paint gives excellent results; just add water if it is too thick.

commercial stamp pads These are available in a rainbow of colors at stationery, craft supply and specialty stores. Keep them closed with rubber bands and store them upside down.

paint stamp pad Make one using a paint tray with a thin sponge or a few layers of dampened absorbent cloth in it. Rinse it when you are finished and reuse it the next time. The paint stamp pad is helpful when you're printing with your hands, fruits and vegetables, and odds 'n' ends so that you don't get too much paint when you dip.

paint trays Pie plates, old dinner plates, cookie sheets or any other washable trays are good for holding paint.

knife A smooth paring knife or craft knife with a retractable blade works well. Always ask an adult to help.

RUBBINGS

THINGS YOU NEED

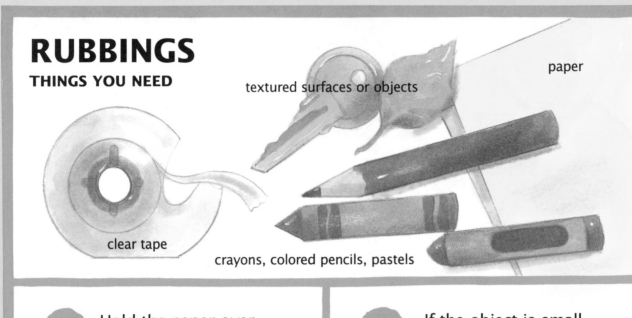

textured surfaces or objects

paper

clear tape

crayons, colored pencils, pastels

1 Hold the paper over the surface or object you want to rub.

2 If the object is small, such as a coin or key, it's helpful to secure it to the tabletop with a small loop of tape.

3 Rub the side of your crayon or pastel over the paper. If you're rubbing with colored pencils, use them on an angle.

Fun ideas to try

⭐ Rub over an object or surface with more than one color of crayon, colored pencil or pastel.

⭐ Rubbings can be used to decorate writing paper, posters, cards and wrapping paper.

⭐ Make some play money by making rubbings of both sides of a coin. Cut them out. Glue one coin rubbing onto lightweight cardboard. Cut this out. Now glue the rubbing of the other side of the coin to the back.

⭐ Look for interesting surfaces to rub. Here are some ideas to get you started: puzzle pieces, keys, coins, pavement, bark, leaves, fabric, toys, shells.

HAND PRINTS

THINGS YOU NEED

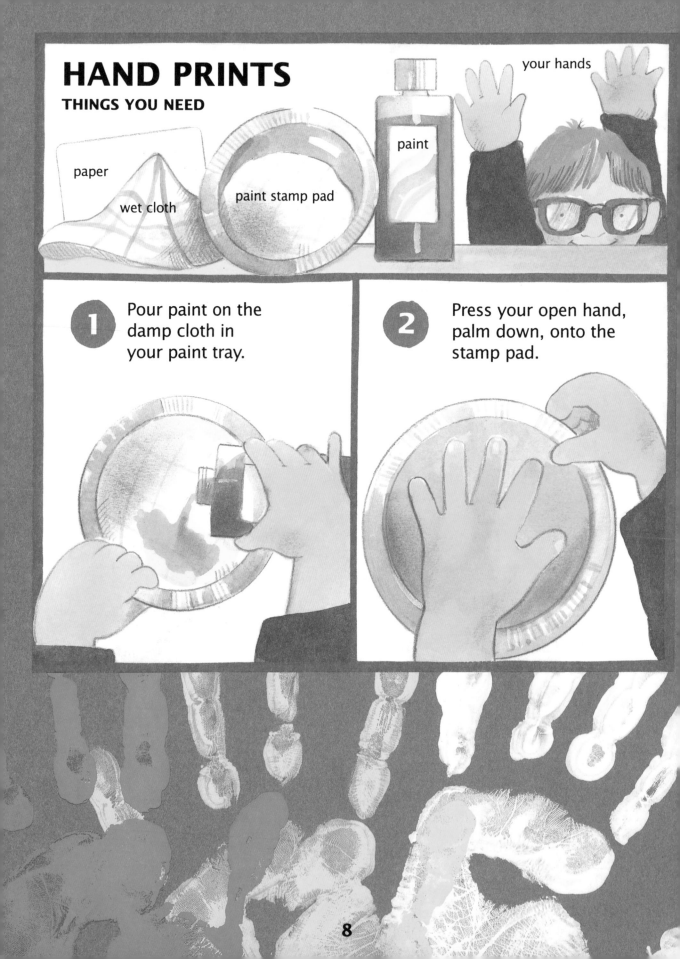

paper

wet cloth

paint stamp pad

paint

your hands

1 Pour paint on the damp cloth in your paint tray.

2 Press your open hand, palm down, onto the stamp pad.

3 Print with your hand, pressing evenly so all parts are touching the paper.

4 Wipe your hand on the wet cloth.

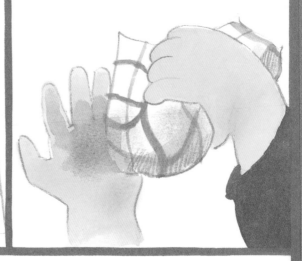

Fun ideas to try

♥ Experiment with different parts of your hand; fingertips, fist, thumb or knuckles.

♥ If you want to make "thumbuddies," use an ink stamp pad to print your thumb. Add a face, arms and legs with a pen or marker.

♥ How about sending a family hand portrait to relatives or friends? Everyone in your family could press their hand prints on a large sheet of paper.

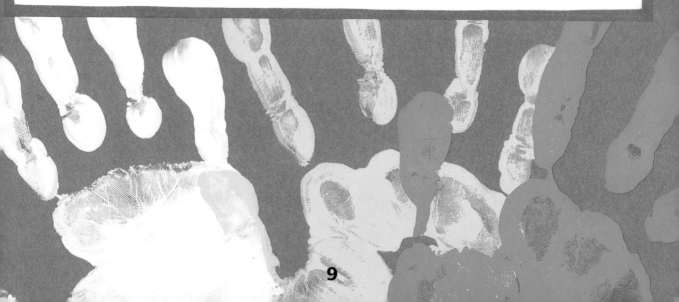

VEGETABLE AND FRUIT PRINTS

THINGS YOU NEED

vegetables and fruits

paring knife

paint stamp pad

paper

paint

1 Pour paint on the damp cloth in the paint tray.

2 Ask an adult to help you cut your fruit or vegetable in half. Try to cut it smoothly.

3 Press the cut side down onto the paint stamp pad.

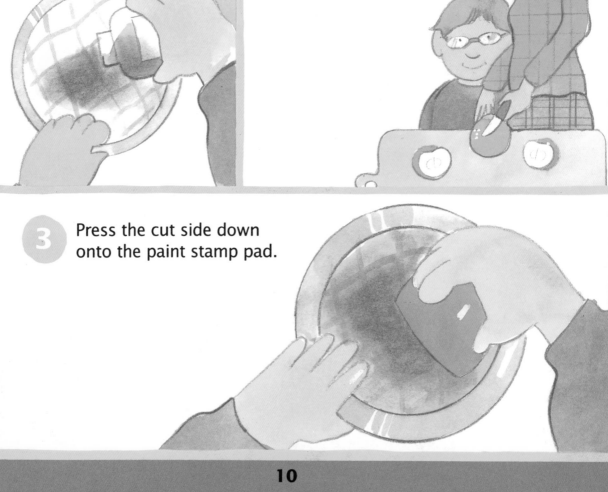

4 Print on your paper. Repeat the print as often as you like to make a design.

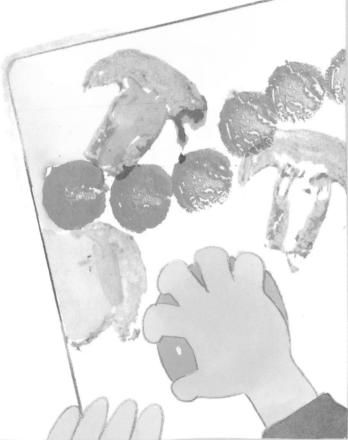

5 Rinse the fruit or vegetable if you want to change the color of paint. When you're finished printing, put the leftovers in the composter.

POTATO PRINTING

THINGS YOU NEED

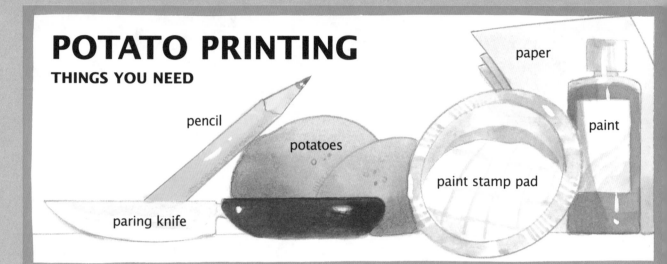

paper

pencil

potatoes

paint

paint stamp pad

paring knife

1 Ask an adult to help you cut your potato in half. Make sure the surface is smooth so that it will print evenly.

2 Draw a design on your potato. Or draw a design on a piece of paper, cut it out and place it on the potato. Your printed image will be the reverse of what's on your potato. This is important to remember when printing letters.

3 Ask an adult to help you cut your potato design. Do not undercut the design, or the edges will be weak.

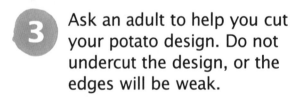

well cut edges

poorly cut edges

4 Pour paint on the damp cloth in the paint stamp pad. Press the cut side of the potato down onto it.

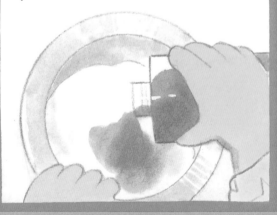

5 Print on newspaper or scrap paper first to see if you are pleased with your design. Change it if you like or start printing on your good paper.

6 Rinse the potato when you want to change the color of paint. Be sure to compost the leftovers. Potatoes don't keep for long once they are cut, but you can use yours for a second day if you wrap it tightly in plastic and put it in the fridge.

SPONGE PRINTING

THINGS YOU NEED

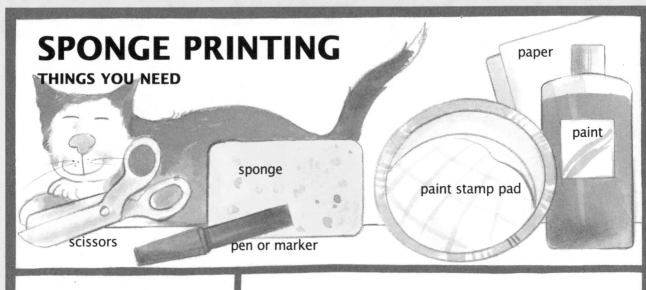

paper

paint

paint stamp pad

sponge

pen or marker

scissors

1 Draw a shape on your sponge.

2 Ask an adult to help you cut out your design.

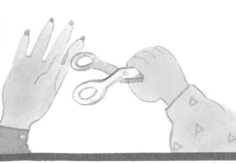

3 Wet your sponge shape with water then squeeze it out. Now print it on newspaper or scrap paper — you'll see the water print. If it doesn't look right, trim your sponge some more.

4 Pour a little paint into the tray. Dip the sponge lightly into the paint.

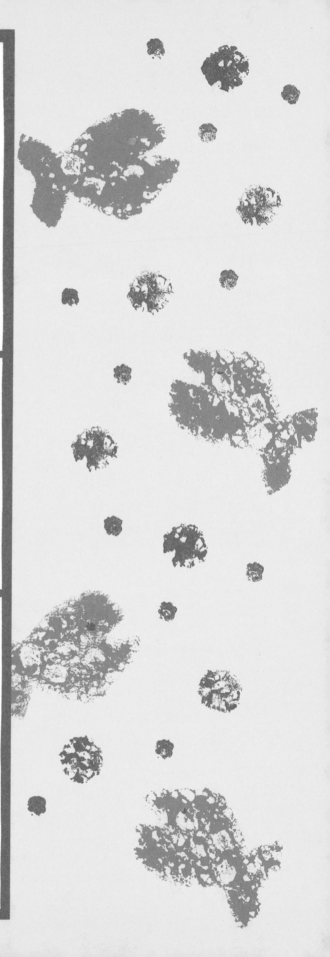

5 Print on your good paper. Push down gently so that the paint does not smear.

6 Rinse the sponge well if you want to print with a different color of paint, or before putting it away. It will last a long time.

Fun ideas to try

⭐ Glue small, dry pieces of sponge onto a wooden block or jar lid. Can you make an animal paw print or a face?

⭐ Make some gift wrap and matching cards.

⭐ Sponges come in many different textures. Try some with very small holes and some with large holes.

CARDBOARD PRINTING

THINGS YOU NEED

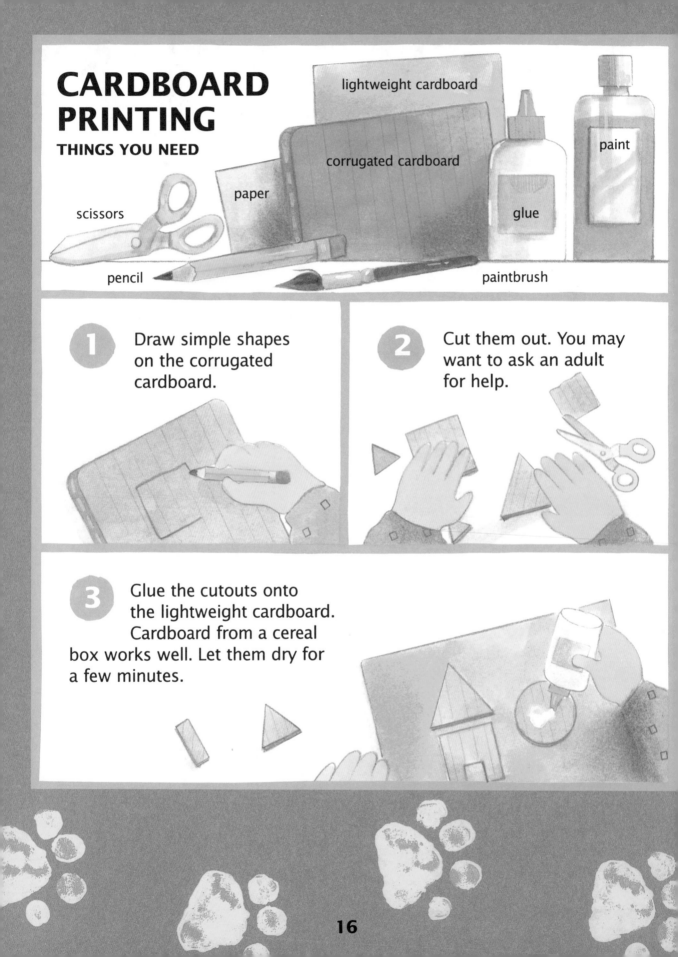

lightweight cardboard

corrugated cardboard

paper

paint

scissors

glue

pencil

paintbrush

1 Draw simple shapes on the corrugated cardboard.

2 Cut them out. You may want to ask an adult for help.

3 Glue the cutouts onto the lightweight cardboard. Cardboard from a cereal box works well. Let them dry for a few minutes.

4 Using the paintbrush, apply paint to the corrugated cardboard cutouts. If some of the paint dries before you get a chance to print it, reapply paint or brush on a little water.

5 Carefully place your printing paper on top of the cardboard. While holding the paper with one hand, smooth over it with your other hand.

6 Lift the paper. Reapply paint and repeat as often as you wish.

Fun ideas to try

💜 Make smaller designs by cutting out shapes and gluing them onto a wooden block or jar lid. Apply the paint with a brush and press down on paper to print.

💜 Strip the top layer off the corrugated cardboard. Apply paint and print a striped design.

PIPE CLEANER PRINTS

THINGS YOU NEED

pipe cleaners

paint

paint stamp pad

paper

Popsicle stick

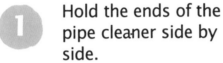

1 Hold the ends of the pipe cleaner side by side.

2 Twist them together. This will give you a little "tail."

3 Bend the pipe cleaner into a shape. Bend the tail upward.

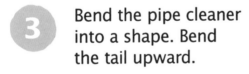

4 Pour some paint into the tray. Holding onto the pipe cleaner tail, dip your shape into the paint.

5 Apply the shape to the paper. If all parts of the pipe cleaner do not touch the paper, gently push down along the pipe cleaner with the Popsicle stick or your fingers.

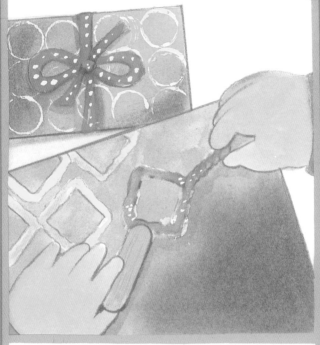

6 Rinse the pipe cleaner when you want to print with another color of paint, or when you are ready to put it away.

STRING PRINTS

THINGS YOU NEED

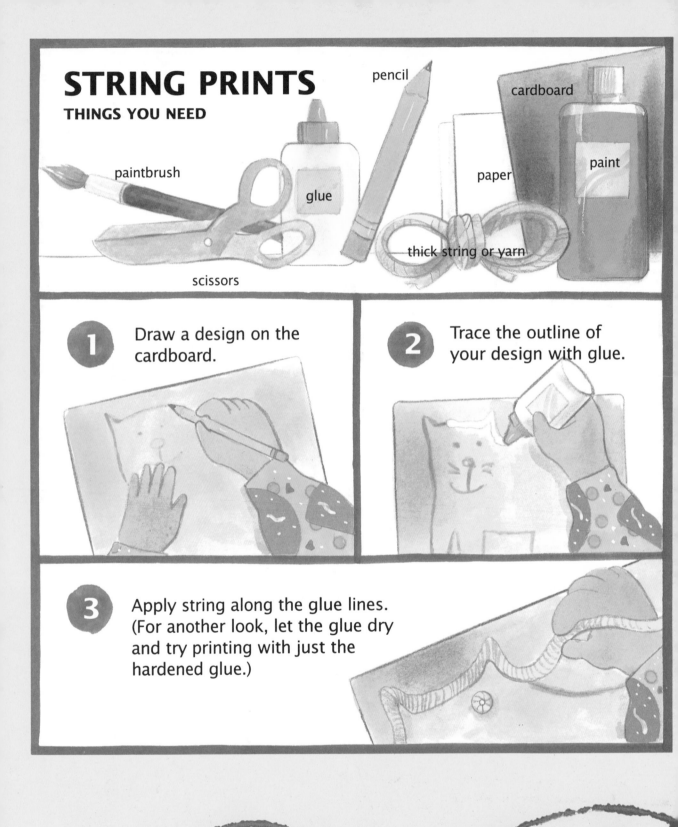

pencil

cardboard

paintbrush

paint

glue

paper

thick string or yarn

scissors

1 Draw a design on the cardboard.

2 Trace the outline of your design with glue.

3 Apply string along the glue lines. (For another look, let the glue dry and try printing with just the hardened glue.)

4 Do not overlap the string. If you come to a spot where the string must cross over another string, cut it and start a new piece on the other side. Let it dry for at least 15 minutes.

5 Use the paintbrush to apply paint to the string. You may need to put extra paint on the first time because the string will absorb some of it.

6 Put your sheet of paper on the design. Hold the paper in place with one hand and smooth over your design with your other hand.

7 Lift the paper and admire your string print.

STENCILING AND SPLATTER PRINTS

THINGS YOU NEED

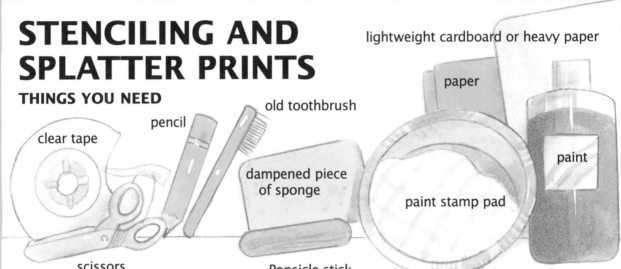

lightweight cardboard or heavy paper

paper

old toothbrush

pencil

clear tape

paint

dampened piece of sponge

paint stamp pad

scissors

Popsicle stick

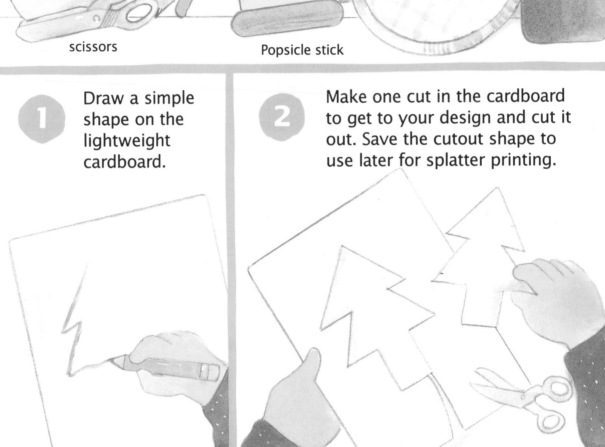

1 Draw a simple shape on the lightweight cardboard.

2 Make one cut in the cardboard to get to your design and cut it out. Save the cutout shape to use later for splatter printing.

3 Tape over the cut you made so that there is no opening in the cardboard. This will be your stencil.

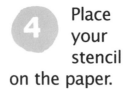

4 Place your stencil on the paper.

5 Hold the stencil very still as you dab paint inside it with the sponge.

6 Try splatter printing your stencil. Dip the bristles of the toothbrush into the paint. Hold the toothbrush with the bristles facing down. Use the Popsicle stick to carefully flick paint over your stencil.

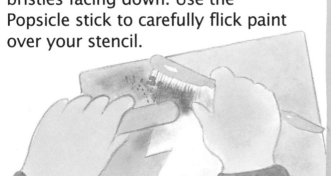

7 Put the cutout from your stencil on a piece of paper and sponge or splatter paint around it for a whole new look.

ERASER PRINTS

THINGS YOU NEED

paper

craft knife

ink stamp pad

gum eraser

pencil

1 Use the pencil to trace the outline of your eraser on a small piece of paper. Press hard.

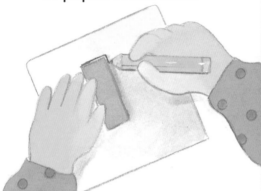

2 Draw a design inside the outline on your paper. If you are drawing letters, make them wide.

3 Place the drawing face down on the eraser. Pressing hard, scribble back and forth until the outlined area is filled in. Be careful not to move the paper as you scribble.

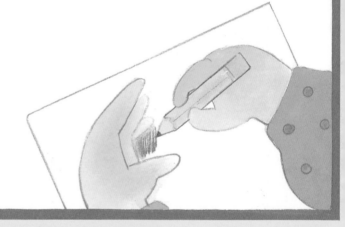

4 Lift the paper. Your design should now be on the eraser, too. It will be backward, but it will print the right way.

5 Ask an adult to help you cut out your design with a craft knife. Do not undercut the design or the edges may break.

well cut edges

poorly cut edges

6 Press the eraser down on the ink stamp pad a few times then stamp it on scrap paper. If you're not happy with your design, do some more cutting.

7 Print on your good paper. Before using a different color on your eraser, stamp it over and over on scrap paper to get rid of all the ink.

Fun ideas to try

🖤 Ask an adult to help you cut a small shape into an un-used pencil eraser. Try a tiny moon, star, heart or face.

GIFT BOXES

THINGS YOU NEED

printing supplies

glue

an empty lightweight cardboard box

1 Carefully open both ends of the box. Run your fingers down the glued side seam to undo it.

2 Lay the box flat, inside up, on your work surface.

3 Print the box using any of the methods you've learned in this book.

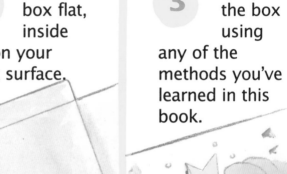

4 Glue the side seam together. You will need to hold it for a couple of minutes.

5 Glue the bottom of the box together and hold it for awhile.

6 Use the tab closure on the top to open and close your inside-out gift box. It's reusable.

GIFT BAGS

THINGS YOU NEED

paper bags

printing supplies

scissors

1 If the bag is plain, simply lay it flat and print one side at a time.

2 If the bag is already printed on the outside, cut down one side of the bag and cut out the bottom. Lay it flat and print the plain side.

3 Use the paper to wrap your gift, or put the gift inside the bag.

PRINTS TO WEAR

THINGS YOU NEED

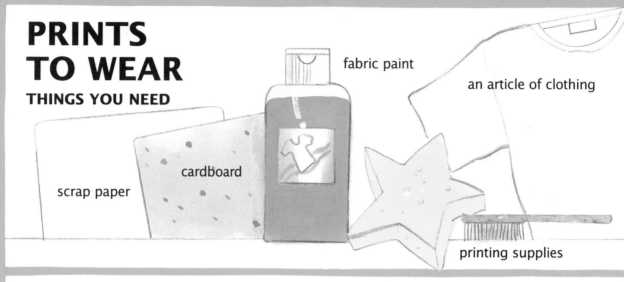

fabric paint

an article of clothing

scrap paper

cardboard

printing supplies

1 Your article of clothing should be washed and smooth for printing. You don't need to wash shoes or laces.

Put cardboard in between the two layers of fabric for T-shirts and shorts.

Tape the ends of shoelaces to the work table.

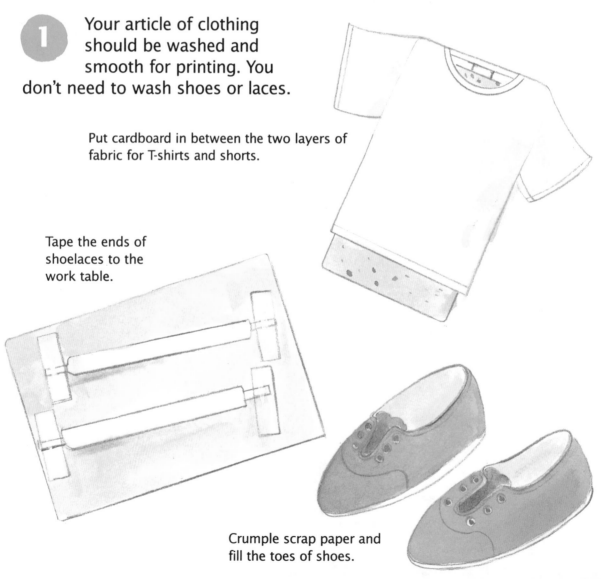

Crumple scrap paper and fill the toes of shoes.

2 Use your favorite printing method and print with fabric paint instead of tempera. Try hand, sponge or potato printing on your T-shirt. Splatter or sponge print your shoes. Use pencil erasers or finger printing on your laces. Always try your design on scrap paper first.

3 To make sure the fabric paint stays on your clothing, cover the printed area with a clean cotton cloth and ask an adult to help you iron it at a hot setting. Shoes can be put in a hot clothes dryer for a few minutes.

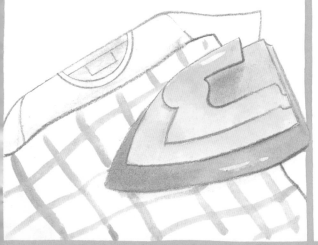

Fun ideas to try

⭐ Print a gift of clothing for a parent, grandparent or friend.
⭐ Print on fabric grocery bags, lunch bags or cloth napkins.

IT'S A PARTY!

Here are some ideas to make your party a stamping good time!

Print your own invitations. If you have a party theme, make designs to match it. Blank 13 x 20 cm (5 x 8 inch) index cards are a good size to use. They come in different colors at stationery stores. Fold them in half and print. Construction paper works well, too. While you're at it, decorate napkins, party hats and grab bags.

Do some printmaking at the party. Make sure each guest has a paint shirt to wear. Have sponges, pipe cleaners and erasers prepared ahead of time for them to use.

Instead of buying your guests grab bags, how about providing T-shirts, shoes or laces for your guests to print? This is a fun party activity. You could even have your guests "sign" each other's shirts with a hand print.

How about a game of "stamp the nose on the clown"? Or, "stamp the leaf on the tree"? Make a large picture on cardboard, cover it with clear plastic and invite each guest to take a turn. Wipe the prints off with a wet cloth when everyone is finished.

ENDLESS PRINTING POSSIBILITIES

Here are some more ideas to keep you printing.

Leaf Prints Place a leaf, vein-side up, on newspaper. Paint lightly over the veins with a sponge or brush. Place it on paper, paint side down. Use scrap paper to cover the leaf and press gently with your hand. Lift the scrap paper and the leaf.

Find and Print Look for lots of different textures and shapes to print with. Use an ink pad or a paint stamp pad to try printing with some of these objects: tissue rolls, corn cobs, cones, corks, cookie cutters, cutlery, crumpled foil or wax paper, jar lids, jar bottoms, the bottoms of old shoes, spools, pom-poms, heads of bolts and screws and thimbles. . .

Plasticine Prints Press a piece of Plasticine or other modeling clay onto a smooth surface. Gently lift it off. Now press the Plasticine over a textured surface such as a wheel on a toy, or use a pencil to poke a design into it. Apply the Plasticine to an ink stamp pad and then onto paper. Don't press too hard. Stamp the Plasticine on scrap paper to get rid of the remaining ink.